The Dragons of Wayward Crescent

For Lydia

ORCHARD BOOKS
338 Euston Road, London NW1 3BH
Orchard Books Australia
Level 17/207 Kent Street, Sydney, NSW 2000

First published in 2009 by Orchard Books

First paperback publication in 2010

ISBN 978 1 40830 234 7 (HB)
ISBN 978 1 84616 611 2 (PB)

Text © Chris d'Lacey 2009
Illustrations © Adam Stower 2009
The rights of Chris d'Lacey to be identified as the author
and Adam Stower to be identified as the illustrator of this
work have been asserted by them in accordance with the
Copyright, Designs and Patents Act, 1988.

A CIP catalogue record for this book
is available from the British Library.
1 3 5 7 9 10 8 6 4 2
Printed in Great Britain
Orchard Books is a division of Hachette Children's Books,
an Hachette UK company.
www.hachette.co.uk

Chris d'Lacey

The Dragons of Wayward Crescent

GLADE

Illustrated by Adam Stower

ORCHARD BOOKS

Chapter One

"Gosh, it's chilly today," Elizabeth Pennykettle said, stamping her feet and blowing on the ends of her fingerless gloves. "Still, these spring weekends are always good for business. How are we doing, Lucy?"

Liz's ten-year-old daughter looked

around the covered market stalls. She'd seen more elephants at a water hole than people shopping today. She looked at the rows of clay dragons on her mother's stall then glanced at the open cash tin, which was on an upturned fruit crate beside her. There was a ten-pound note and some coins in it. "We've sold two," she said glumly.

"Well, that's two better than none at all," said Liz.

Lucy sighed and pulled on the braids of her bobble hat. She was about to reply when the clock in the tower of the library building gave out three distinct bongs. Anyone who didn't live in the market town of Scrubbley would have thought this rather odd, for it was clearly about eleven o'clock in the morning. But to Lucy, who not only knew the whole sequence of bongs but the reason why the clock always chimed incorrectly, it was no surprise at all. It even helped reinforce what she'd been planning to say: "Mum, we've been standing here for over an hour. I hate doing the market on freezing cold days. My toes are cold. And I think I've got chilblains – on my knees!"

"Well, I'm sorry, but I have to earn a living," Liz said. "We have to eat and pay the bills like anyone else. Making and selling clay dragons is what I do. If you can think of a better job for me, speak up." With that, she leaned across the stall and rearranged a number of her spiky green creations, moving some that had been at the back much closer to the front and placing others in little clusters, on stands.

Another spill of cold air ran though the marketplace, flapping the bunting on the roofs of the stalls. Lucy shivered and let her hands drift towards a female dragon in the corner of the table nearest her. It was sitting up on its back legs and tail as most of the Pennykettle dragons did. Nearly all of Liz's dragons were characterised in some way. They carried cricket bats or wore a chef's hat, for instance. The dragon nearest Lucy was slightly different. It had a scarf of ivy leaves around its neck. In truth, it was rather an ordinary-looking sculpture. Yet it was the most special of any on the stall. For this pretty little creature was only acting like a piece of solid clay, the way it had been taught to do in human company. But at any given moment it could soften its scales, lift its wings, make fire in the back of its throat and fly. It was real and barely three weeks old. Its name was Glade.

Lucy stretched the sleeve of her coat from her wrist and held the gap in front of Glade's snout.

Then she made a strange kind of grunting sound, which to most people would have sounded like she had a bad cold. Actually, it was an ancient language called dragontongue, which Lucy and her mother had been able to speak since birth. To Glade's ears the grunt translated as *Hrrr*, which could be interpreted in any number of ways, but which Glade understood to mean, "Blow, will you?"

With a quick snuffle, Glade snorted a blast of air, warming Lucy's forearm instantly.

"Hey," said Liz, catching sight of what was happening. "What have I told you about using the special dragons in public?" She looked around quickly to check that no one

was watching the stall. The market trader next to them was bellowing out special offers on his tapestry kits. Fortunately, he was drawing most people's attention.

"You said we could bring Glade here," Lucy argued.

"I didn't say we could show the world our secrets, did I?"

Lucy folded her arms. "Then why have we brought her?" This, Lucy thought, was a fair argument. She had lived with these dragons all her life. She knew the rules. And all the secrets. (Well, nearly all the secrets.) Her mother made dragons that came alive (sometimes). To achieve this, Liz used the powers of a magical snowball that never melted in her hands but would turn to water inside a dragon's snout. From this water the dragon would create its life spirit, or 'fire tear'. The exact process was a mystery, even to Lucy, but she did know that special dragons had to be protected from prying eyes, which was why it was so unusual for a special one to leave their house in Wayward Crescent. "Well?" Lucy pressed.

Liz ran her fingers along Glade's spine. "She wanted to come."

Lucy wrinkled her nose. "Why?"

There was a plain white tablecloth draped over the stall. Liz picked up the hem and let it run through her fingers. "Dragons are very sensitive. I think she believes her destiny is here."

"On the market?" That didn't make sense to Lucy at all. "But… you make them to help us, in the house."

"True," Liz said. "But lately I've been thinking about how lucky we

13

are to have our dragons and how good it would be if we could share them with other people sometimes."

Lucy shifted closer and whispered like a spy. "Mum, if we share them, people will know they're real. Then scientists will come to the house and take away the snowball and do experiments on it. They'd treat us like…"

"Aliens. Yes, I know," Liz said, and there was suddenly a twinkle of intense bright violet at the centre of her normally placid green eyes. "All the same, I have to find out why Glade wants to be here. Anyway, shush, we'll talk about this later. I think we've got customers."

Lucy looked up to see an enthusiastic young girl in a duffel coat approaching. She was dragging along a slightly breathless woman. "Mum, look! Pottery dragons! Can I have one? Please?"

The mother drew up to the stall. She adjusted the strap of her bag and said a quiet hello to Liz and Lucy. "Gosh, they're beautiful. Did you make them yourself?"

"In a studio, in my house," Liz replied.

Lucy said proudly, "It's called the Dragons' Den."

The woman smiled and glanced at a couple of price tags. "All right, Melanie, you can have one. How about this ballerina one, here?"

She pointed at a dragon in a pale pink tutu.

The girl put a finger to her lip and shook her head.

"These are very popular," said Liz, stroking a baby emerging from its egg.

The girl's eyes continued to scan the sculptures. "I like that one..." she said, pointing to a dragon that was playing a recorder.

"Oh, yes," laughed her mum. "Maybe it could help you with your music lessons?"

The girl nodded. "But I really want that one," she said and pointed firmly at Glade.

Lucy made a sound as if she'd swallowed a fly.

"Why that one?" asked Liz.

The girl thought for a moment. "I like her. She's got kind eyes."

Chapter 2

"Glade's not for sale," Lucy said with a start.

"Glade? That's a lovely name," said the mother.

"I can't have her?" asked the girl. Her young face crumpled up in disappointment.

Lucy picked Glade up as if to lay claim to her. But Liz immediately took her out of Lucy's hands. "What Lucy means is, we don't have a gift box for this one. So strictly speaking she's not available."

"Oh, we don't mind about a box, do we, Mel?" Melanie's mother said with an understanding smile.

"No," said Melanie. "Can I hold her?"

Liz smiled and handed Glade over.

Lucy felt as if her lungs had turned to stone. She watched Melanie hold the dragon close to her heart, cradling Glade as if she were a baby.

"I'd be happy to pay the full

price," said Melanie's mother, "box or no box." She reached into her bag and unclipped her purse.

Liz raised a hand and waited till the woman's gaze met hers. Lucy curled her fingers in hope. She could see that Liz's eyes were changing to violet. Liz was going to use her magical powers to make the woman change her mind.

But in fact Liz said, "I really think you ought to have a box. These dragons are much more collectable with them. Besides, I like to paint the buyer's name – Melanie, isn't it? – on the tail. You do understand, don't you?"

Like a robot, the woman closed her purse. "Erm, yes," she said

dizzily. "That would be lovely...
I think."

That was far too chancy for Lucy.
She bit her lip and stared like

a demon at the girl, trying to turn her own eyes violet, hoping that she might bend Melanie's will and persuade her to give Glade back. To her dismay, the magic only half-worked. The girl returned Glade to the stall, but kept her hands cupped around her wings.

"So, should we come back next week?" asked her mother.

"Where do you live?" asked Liz.

"Orchid Close. Number 7."

"Orchid Close?" gasped Lucy. That was the road next to Wayward Crescent.

"You know it?"

"We're practically neighbours," said Liz. She leaned forward and picked Glade up. "We'll take the

dragon for now. I'll sort
out a box and we'll
pop round…tomorrow,
perhaps?"

"Come for tea," the
woman said.

"Thank you," said
Liz. "That's very kind."
She glanced at Melanie,
who seemed a little uncertain.

"Mum, shouldn't we tell them
about…?"

"Oh, yes," said her mum, looking
anxious. "Melanie's grandad lives
with us. He's… Well, he can be a
little, erm, eccentric."

"What does that mean?" asked
Lucy.

Her mother touched Glade's ears.

Lucy noticed that the dragon had pricked them slightly. Liz said, "Well, we'll find out, won't we?"

Melanie's mother parted her lips. She looked grateful for Liz's kind response. "Shall we say four o'clock?"

"We'll be there, on the dot," said Liz.

And with that, they waved Melanie and her mother goodbye.

Lucy waited until they were well out of earshot then said from the side of her mouth, "Good plan, Mum. Brilliant idea."

"Plan?" said Liz.

"You're going to take Glade home and make a replica, aren't you? You're going to take that round instead."

Liz shook her head. "I'd never get a replica glazed in time. We need to take Glade home and prepare her, though."

"What? You're really going to sell her? You're going to paint her tail and hand her over?"

Liz thought for a moment. "Well, she will be going to Melanie's house, but I don't think she's going to be Melanie's dragon." She lifted Glade from the tablecloth and turned her round. "Show Lucy what you just showed me."

Glade flicked her tail straight

25

then rearranged the scales until Lucy could clearly see a word spelled out.

"There. What do you make of that?" asked Liz.

Lucy gripped the edge of the stall. This was getting worse. The word that Glade had made was not 'Melanie'.

It was 'Grandad'.

Chapter 3

All the way home, Lucy thought about the description of Melanie's grandad. Yet it was only when they stepped into the hall at Wayward Crescent that she thought to ask again, "Mum, what exactly does 'eccentric' mean?"

"Look it up," said Liz. "If you want to find out anything in this world you should consult a good book. In this case, the dictionary."

Lucy stopped in the hall by the front-room door. She looked in, frowning at the small stack of books in the alcove. The dictionary was heavy and high up – and boring. She chewed her lip a moment then carried Glade through to the kitchen and put her down on the table, all the while calling out for a dragon named Gruffen to join them.

Gruffen came whizzing in. He was a guard dragon by trade, though not a very good one. When Gruffen had been made, he'd come with a book of 'instructions', which was really a sort of alphabetical guide to being a dragon. Lucy, being a human, and a lazy one at that, decided to ask him to look up 'eccentric', hoping he'd find an answer for her.

Like any Pennykettle dragon, Gruffen did his best to help. It was a difficult word, though, and he had to ask Lucy to spell it.

Spelling. Not Lucy's best subject at school. "E, G, G, erm, S, erm, N…TRICK," she said.

Gruffen blew some dust off his book and flipped through it. Not surprisingly, the word wasn't there,

for it had nothing whatsoever to do with dragons (not to mention the fact that Lucy had hopelessly misspelled it). He did find 'Eggs', though. "Would that be any good?" he hurred.

"Useless," Lucy tutted, flopping down into a chair.

Gruffen read the entry to himself, anyway. It looked quite interesting to him. *Eggs*, it said. *Ancient means of dragon birth and sometimes of human-like children, touched by the spark of a dragon.* Hmm. He looked thoughtfully at Lucy and closed the book.

Just then, an elderly gentleman appeared at the back door. His bony knuckle rapped the glass. Gruffen,

Glade and the listening dragon that always sat on top of the fridge immediately adopted their solid form.

Lucy gave a thin groan. The caller was their annoying next-door neighbour, Henry Bacon. "Mum, Count Dracula's arrived!"

"What?" her mum shouted, distantly.

"There's an old grey vampire on our threshold," Lucy said (quietly, to herself). That was how Mr Bacon looked to her, anyway. She opened the door and invited him in.

"Your mother home, child?"

Mr Bacon always spoke to Lucy like this. One day she was determined to respond in similar fashion saying, "Yes, she's upstairs, old man." On this occasion, however, she was quite polite – but then she did have a reason. Henry was a librarian. He knew about words. So Lucy put on her best little-girl voice and said, "Erm, yes, Mum's home. Would you like a cup of tea?"

Unnerved by this uncommonly warm reception, Henry sat down and mumbled, "Very well. One sugar – and not too much milk."

Lucy marched to the sink and filled the kettle. "Mr Bacon, what does 'eggsntrick' mean?"

"Eccentric," he tutted. "It's spelled with a double 'c', child."

Lucy ground her teeth. She thought, *Shall I put a squirt of washing-up liquid in his tea? Better not.* "Does it mean clever?"

"No. It means 'odd' or 'peculiar'. Eccentric people are usually considered to be slightly barmy."

"Barmy?!" Lucy gasped. "You mean, like—"

'You', she was about to say, had Liz not walked in and cut her off. "Good. I see Lucy's put the kettle on. What can we do for you, Henry?"

"Is that ivy?" he asked, pointing at the leaves around Glade's neck.

"Yes," Liz said. "It suits her, don't you think?"

"Can't bear the stuff," said Henry. "Smothers your brickwork and gets under your roof. It's in my shed, Mrs P, digging its ghastly shoots between my slates. Coming from a branch on your side, I think. Need your permission to hack it all back."

Before Liz could comment, Lucy grabbed her by the wrist and turned her away. "Mu-um, you'd better look at Glade," she hissed.

Liz glanced back. The ivy around Glade's neck was glowing a faint, but definite, fiery red. And she had softened her tail just enough to flick it, temperamentally, from side to side.

Henry, being an aged human, and disbelieving of any form of movement in a 'clay' sculpture, did not see the tail, but he had seen the change in colour of the ivy.

"Good Lord," he said. "That thing's glowing."

Lucy breathed in slowly. Glade wasn't going to like being called a 'thing'. She could already see the dragon's youthful claws emerging. And was that a hint of smoke in her nostrils?

Liz was swift to react. She scooped Glade up and said to Henry, "Her ivy has been dusted with mood paint."

"What?" he blustered.

"She changes colour according to your mood. Red for anger. You really ought to calm down, Henry."

"Nonsense. Let me look at it again," he said.

"I don't think that's a good idea," said Lucy, squeezing the words from the side of her mouth.

Liz shrugged and held Glade close to Henry's face.

"Hmm," he went, and tinked her nose with his fingernail.

In a move so fast that Henry felt nothing but a mild tickle, Glade softened her paws and put two claws up his hairy nostrils. Immediately, Henry's nose hairs began to grow.

And grow.

And grow.

And grow.

And, well, grow.

"What the—? What's happening?" he cried, as the hairs began to reach the bottom of his chin. Some were even curling up towards his ears.

He jumped up and glanced in the kitchen mirror. "Arrgh! I've turned into a walrus!" And before anyone could speak he'd dashed out of the kitchen and was hurtling back towards his own house.

"Well, now at least we know what Glade's good at," said Liz.

Lucy's mouth was still wide open in shock.

Liz smiled and said, "Do you want to demonstrate on something less…human, Glade?"

The little dragon softened and looked around. *Hrrr*, she went and flew to the vegetable rack. She came back with a small potato. She turned it between her front paws for a second, then *hurred* on one end.

Suddenly, a tiny green shoot popped sideways out of the potato.

"Wow," gasped Lucy.

Glade's eyes turned a sweet shade of violet. *Hrrr*, she went again and breathed on the shoot, which began to thicken and strengthen and slowly turn upwards. It had grown about ten or fifteen millimetres in length when the tip wiggled and split. It peeled into four and out of its centre came a small white flower.

"WOW!" Lucy said, even louder this time. "She grows things." She blinked in amazement as another shoot popped out of the potato. "So, what's she going to do when she goes to Melanie's house?"

Liz picked Glade up and kissed

her. "Something wonderful," she whispered proudly.

Lucy hummed and tapped her foot. She wasn't so sure. If Melanie's grandad was anything like Henry Bacon, there was going to be a LOT of trouble…

Chapter 4

Even so, the next day, Liz wrapped Glade in straw and placed her inside a Pennykettle gift box, ready to go to Melanie's house.

By now, the young dragon had been educated in the ways of the human world. She had been told she must always be good and helpful, but that she must act wisely and, above all, secretly. She was never to turn real, for instance, if there was ever any chance of humans seeing her. Liz explained that although it was difficult for most human people to see a dragon moving, they might still suspect. And that was just as bad. So, for the rest of that day, Liz and Lucy (and some of the other house dragons) practised creeping up on Glade, until she could freeze in an instant. She was ready.

Just before she was packed, Liz taught her another important lesson. "Listen to me," she said softly, looking down into the box before she put the last clutch of straw over Glade's head.

The young dragon sloped her violet eyes upwards.

"I don't know why you need to go to Melanie's house or what you need to do for her grandad, but it might be sad."

"Sad?" said Lucy. She sat back in alarm. She knew what her mother was about to say.

"No matter how troubled things become," Liz said. "You must never cry your fire tear. If you do, you will never be able to turn real again. Do you understand?"

There was a rustle of straw inside the box. A dragon's tail twitching, perhaps. Glade nodded slightly.

"All right. Are you comfortable?"

Glade burrowed down like a gerbil. A muffled *hufffrrr* suggested she was snug.

"Good. Then off we go."

* * *

It took less than five minutes to walk along the Crescent and take the looping turn into Orchid Close. The houses were almost identical in aspect, with long, leafy gardens and broad, welcoming windows. Lucy was able to take comfort in that. At least Glade was going somewhere like home.

Melanie had seen them coming and already had the front door open, waiting. Without breaking her stride, Liz stepped inside and said hello.

Melanie's mother appeared. She was wearing a blue striped apron. The sweet smell of baked cake followed her down the hall. She had a tiny blob of cake mix on her cheek. "Lovely to see you. Thanks so much for coming. I'm Rachel, by the way. Pops is in the lounge."

"Pops?" said Lucy.

"It's what Mum calls Grandad," Melanie explained.

Lucy nodded. Her fingers closed more tightly around Glade's box.

Coats were taken, shoes were kicked off and everyone shuffled into a large, comfortable room somehow made smaller by its chunky brown carpet and woven fabric sofa. There was an empty bird cage near the fire. Lucy noticed that its door was ajar and looked around quickly for signs of a budgie on the curtain pelmet or the picture rails. There was none. But in the chair beside the cage was an elderly man. He was slumped to one side, asleep. The folds of his chin were stacking against his shoulder. Lucy noticed how they wobbled whenever he snored.

"Oh, dear. He's gone again," Rachel said. "He does this, I'm afraid. On and off like a lighthouse. Do sit down."

"Shall I wake him?" asked Melanie, touching the man's arm. "Grandad?" She shook him gently.

Pops snorted loudly and turned in
his chair. He gave a rasping cough
and jerked to attention. "Uh, I was

watching that," he said. His glazed eyes travelled to the TV screen, but it wasn't even on.

"Pops, this is Melanie's new friend," said Rachel, talking louder than she normally would. "The one who's bringing her a dragon, remember?"

The old man fiddled with his hearing aid. "Digging? What's that about digging?"

Melanie rolled her eyes. "Not digging, Grandad, DRAGON," she shouted.

"Oh," said Pops. He sat back and nodded as though he understood.

"He's a keen gardener," Rachel said quietly, perching herself on the arm of a chair. "At least he was, until his illness. He still likes to potter about in his greenhouse, but we have to keep a careful eye on him. He gets confused sometimes, as you've discovered."

"Can I see my dragon now?" asked Melanie. She kneeled in front of Lucy and reached out her hands. Reluctantly, Lucy gave her the box.

Melanie opened it and slid Glade out. "Look!" she said proudly, placing Glade on the coffee table. "Look, Grandad, a new dragon!"

The old man gave a slight start.

49

"Has it come from the bottom of the garden?"

Melanie sighed and picked a twist of loose straw off Glade's tail. "No, Grandad. This lady made it. We bought it at the market yesterday."

"Oh," he said. "I did ask, you know."

"Asked what?" queried Rachel, frowning at him.

He took a deep swallow. "For them. Down the garden."

"Them? What are you talking about, Pops?"

The old man stared at Glade.

"It's not a fairy," said Lucy, getting his drift.

"Eh? What's that? What's hairy?" he said.

Rachel sighed. "Nothing, Pops. Nothing's hairy. Would you like a sandwich? Mrs Pennykettle and her daughter are staying for tea."

"Kettle? Oh, yes, put the kettle on," he said.

Rachel threw up her hands. "I'm sorry. It's going to be like this all afternoon, I'm afraid."

"It's all right," Liz said. "May I ask him a question?"

"If you don't mind a silly answer. Be my guest. Call him Pops, if you like. He'll respond to that."

Liz shuffled forward to the front of the sofa. "Do you like the dragon, Pops?"

Melanie's grandad cast his eyes down. "Does it fly?" he whispered.

He tucked his arms into his sides and flapped his fingers. Melanie burst out laughing. But Lucy's expression was deadly serious. She could see her mother's eyes twinkling violet. What's more, Liz had just answered Pops in dragontongue, though to everyone else it would have sounded like a cough. "Sometimes. If you dream it," she'd said.

Lucy held her breath, wondering if the old man would understand. She saw him frown and tilt his head, the way dogs often did when they knew their humans were trying to communicate.

Pops let his gaze fall on Glade again. "Glowing," he said.

"Hhh!" gasped Melanie. "Look, she changes colour!"

Sure enough, the ivy around Glade's neck had relaxed into a definite soft bluey-green.

"Yes, she's a mood dragon – among other things," Liz said.

"That is wonderful," Rachel added. "So what mood is bluey-green, do you think?"

"Happy!" cried Melanie, clapping her hands. "Oh, thank you, thank you for bringing me this dragon."

"I'll echo that," Rachel said, standing up. "Now, time we had something to eat. I'm going to finish in the kitchen and set the table. Melanie, why don't you take Lucy upstairs and show her your other dragons."

"Yes," Melanie said, jumping up quickly. "Would you like to?"

"Of course she would," said Liz. "Lucy adores dragons, don't you?"

Lucy couldn't take her eyes off Glade. She was desperate to send her a whispered *hrrr*, mainly to ask if she was indeed happy, because what Lucy had felt when she'd seen the ivy turn blue was that Glade was feeling sad.

But why?

"Come on," said Melanie and took Lucy's hand.

Lucy nodded. She *was* quite interested to see the dragons. As she got up, she saw that Glade's ivy had returned to green, blending in with her natural glaze. The dragon was peaceful and in no danger of shedding her fire tear.

And Melanie's grandad was once again asleep.

Chapter 5

Melanie's bedroom was a mess of clothes and toys. She had a dressing table, just like Lucy did. And a television, just like Lucy didn't. Lucy felt quite envious about that. The room was also wider than Lucy's, with a spare bed on one side, and a cluster of velvety cushions by its headboard. "That's Jenny's bed. She's my big sister," said Melanie. "She goes to boarding school. My dad's quite rich. He's an officer on a ship. He's away a lot. What does your dad do?"

This was a question Lucy always dreaded. "I don't have a dad," she said, looking away.

Melanie chewed her lip. "Oh, sorry."

Lucy gave her an 'it's all right' smile. She did have a dad, but it was hard to explain. He was, well… She glanced at the dressing table. There were four or five dragon models on it.

"This is Merlin," said Melanie,

rushing across and picking up a scarlet one with gold jewelled eyes. "He's the King of Vermania. That's a place I made up. And the blue one is…"

She went on to name them all.

Lucy picked them up in turn. They were beautiful, particularly a fierce grey one with canopy wings that Melanie called Daroth.

But they weren't clay dragons. Not Pennykettles, touched by the magic of the icefire. Not special, like hers.

"Dragon names should start with 'G'," she said. "And it's best if you pronounce it 'Guh'." Most of the dragons in Wayward Crescent were like this. Guh-ruffen. Guh-lade. Guh-uinevere. Lucy had no idea why this was. It just felt natural, as though you were breathing fire into the name when you said it, *Guh...hrrrrr.*

"Wow," said Melanie. Her eyes were like saucers. She held Daroth under her chin. "You know lots about dragons, don't you?"

"A bit," Lucy said modestly.

"They do magic, don't they?"

"Sometimes," said Lucy, not sure how to answer.

"Always," said Melanie. "Can we be friends?"

Lucy felt a pang of hurt in her chest. She didn't have any friends (apart from the dragons). She knew boys and girls at school, of course, but she rarely brought them home or went to their houses. It was just so difficult. They were what they were and she was, well…

"If we were friends, you could sleep over," said Melanie. She pointed at her sister's bed. "We could play games. We could make up stories about our dragons!"

Before Lucy could respond, she heard a noise outside. It was Rachel saying, "Oh, Pops, come back. We're about to have tea. You can't go out now."

Lucy and Melanie went over to the window. Grandad was scuttling down the garden, about to disappear behind a clump of bushes.

"Where's he going?" asked Lucy.

"To his greenhouse, probably."

The two girls stood, side-by-side, looking out. Other than a bluetit taking nuts from a feeder, there was no activity in the garden now. All the movement was in their hearts.

"What's wrong with him?" asked Lucy.

Melanie set Daroth down on the sill. "It's his brain. Mum says there's something growing there. It makes him act funny. I think he's going to die."

"Oh," said Lucy. She felt the space behind her eyes grow warm.

There was a pause, then Melanie said, "Do you think dragon magic would help him get better?"

Lucy thought of Glade. Was this

why she was here, to save the life of Melanie's grandad? But how could she have possibly known that she was needed? Could it be that the Pennykettle dragons were more sensitive than even Lucy or her mum had imagined?

"Tea's ready! Come on down, you two!" Rachel's voice carried high up the stairs.

"OK," said Lucy.

"OK what?" Melanie asked.

"I'll be your friend."

Melanie balled her fists and grinned. "Brilliant."

They giggled, had a hug, then ran downstairs.

As Lucy came into the lounge she saw the table at the far end had been laid with sandwiches. There were cake trays as well and some fancy cups and saucers. Her mother was sitting down, unfolding a serviette.

"Hello, you two. How's Glade settling in?"

"I don't know," said Melanie. "We didn't take her upstairs."

Lucy's eyes went straight to the coffee table. Her heart leaped. Glade wasn't there.

Glances criss-crossed the room. Then Rachel said, "Oh, no." And suddenly, everyone was putting on their shoes and hurrying down the garden.

They found Grandad by the pond. He was on his knees, staring into the water.

"Pops, what are you doing?" Rachel cried. She quickly drew him back from the edge.

"It's not right," he said. "Didn't fly. Not right."

Lucy ran forward and crouched beside him. "Mum!" she gasped, and pointed into the water.

At the bottom of the weed-strewn pond, being nibbled at by a lazy goldfish, was Glade.

Chapter 6

They hauled her out with a long-handled fishing net.

"That's remarkable," said Rachel. "She's completely intact. All those rocks on the bottom and she hasn't chipped a single scale."

"She's got pond weed up her nose,

though," Lucy said, in a manner which her mother always described as 'truculent'.

Liz threw her a warning look.

"Grandad, what were you thinking of?" said Melanie, looking as if she would burst into tears. She stormed away to sit on a garden bench, drying Glade off with dabs of a tissue.

Rachel linked arms and drew her father close. "You're a monkey, aren't you?"

"Monkey?" he repeated, looking glazed.

"A terror in slippers." She gave his cheek a kiss.

"I don't think he meant any harm," said Liz.

"What?" hissed Lucy. "Mum, he chucked Glade in the pond!"

"We don't know that for certain – yet." Liz turned and looked towards the bottom of the garden, at the greenhouse and the ramshackle potting shed.

"When I was girl," Rachel said, gently stroking her father's hand, "he used to tell me stories about the fairies living here. He said they slept 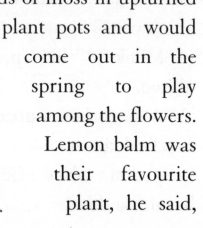 in beds of moss in upturned plant pots and would come out in the spring to play among the flowers. Lemon balm was their favourite plant, he said, because they liked to rub the leaves and smell prettily of lemon. He used to say if I was clever enough to catch sight of a fairy standing on that small stone island in the middle of the pond, all my wishes would come true."

"And did you?" Liz asked.

Rachel bowed her head. "No." She tugged her father's arm. "Is that where you were, Pops? Away with the fairies?"

"Canaries?" he said. "No, they've gone."

Rachel gave an exhausted sigh. "You may have noticed the bird cage in the lounge. We used to have two canaries. He let them out a couple of weeks ago, not realising that the dining-room window was open. They went through it and never came back. Melanie was heartbroken, poor thing. Sometimes life with her grandad isn't easy. Shall we go in now?"

Liz smiled warmly and touched her arm. "Yes, why not. You can't beat a good old cup of tea, can you?"

* * *

Back in the house, they sat Pops at the table and started on the sandwiches. Melanie kept Glade next to her, well away from her grandad's clutches. But as the plates began to empty and the cake was being sliced, Lucy noticed Glade's ivy glowing again, pink. Melanie insisted this was Glade's way of telling her Grandad just how angry she was at getting wet. But Lucy wasn't so sure. It seemed to her that Glade's eyes were following the old man, in that spooky way the eyes of a portrait sometimes did. For some reason that Lucy couldn't quite understand, Glade seemed to be trying to 'connect' with Grandad. Every time the dragon's gaze met with his, her ivy would pulse and he would become very excited, sometimes shouting words at the top of his voice. It was "ONIONS!" the first time. Then "CABBAGES!" Then "SHOVEL!" Rachel tolerated it until halfway through a piece of carrot cake when he barked,

"MANURE!" and spat out a shower of cake crumbs.

"That's it," said Rachel. "You're going to your chair." She stood up and helped him away from the table.

"It talks," Pops gibbered. "It says it's time to plant the runners."

"Well, that's very clever of it," Rachel said. "Now, you just sit quietly and eat the rest of your cake."

She settled Pops down and returned apologetically to the table. "Well, Glade here seems to have caused quite a stir. I haven't seen Pops so fidgety for weeks. Do your dragons always have this effect, Liz?"

"Some more than others," Liz said, smiling.

Lucy raised half an eyebrow and picked a piece of carrot cake off her jumper.

"But you know, the thing is, he's right."

Rachel paused with her fork halfway to her mouth.

"It is the time of year to plant runner beans," said Liz. She lifted her tea cup as if to give a toast, then quietly finished her drink.

Little else was said after that. Tea was over and Liz and Lucy were ready to leave. Rachel accompanied them to the door, calling Melanie to come and say goodbye.

Grandad was dozing again so Melanie took a chance and left Glade on the table.

'Thank yous' were said, hugs were exchanged and Lucy agreed to come back for a sleepover the very next weekend.

"I feel as if we're all going to be

great friends," said Rachel.

"We already are," said Liz. "Let me know how Glade and Pops get on."

"I'm going to take her to my room and hide her!" said Melanie.

And even Lucy had to laugh at that.

When the visitors were out of sight, Rachel closed the door as if she was fitting it into the frame for the very first time. "Well, that was lovely," she said to Melanie. "Will you help with the washing up, please?"

"Yes," said Melanie, heading back into the lounge. "I just want to take Glade upstairs first – hhh!"

To her horror, Glade was not on

the table – but it took less than a second to locate the dragon.

"Oh, Grandad!" Melanie yelled.

The old man was on his feet again, staring through the bars of the canary cage.

There, standing calmly inside it, was Glade.

Chapter 7

"Oh, Pops. Why have you done that?" Even Rachel was annoyed this time.

The old man touched a finger to his lip. "It rang," he said, pointing to the bell inside the cage. "I woke up and..." He pointed to the table, then to Glade.

"Don't fib!" shouted Melanie. "She didn't fly! You put her there! You're horrible, Grandad!"

"No," he said, his face a mixture of confusion and hurt.

But despite his protestations of innocence, Melanie would not believe him. Bursting into tears, she retrieved Glade and ran upstairs with her.

* * *

Glade spent the next few hours under Melanie's bed, put there to keep her away from Grandad. It was dark and dusty and a little uncomfortable (her top knot was poking into the mattress). At one point a spider tried to make its web between the end of her snout and her spiky left ear. She hurred at it gently and the spider scuttled off. Everything was quiet for a while after that.

Grateful for the silence, Glade closed her eyes and thought about the afternoon's events. She was annoyed with herself for breaking the first rule of the Pennykettle code. She had been discovered moving, and that was bad. Luckily for her, everyone had blamed it on the old man. But that made her feel guilty and sorry for him, and even more determined to help.

During tea time, she had made a strong bond with 'Grandad'. It was easy, because he believed in her. He believed she was real. It was a simple matter, then, for her to read his moods. There were a lot of jumbled feelings in his mind. Some about himself, and Rachel, and the garden. He missed planting things and watching them grow. But he was sad most of all about the missing canaries. Glade's mission, she had decided, was to get them back.

So when everyone was out of the room and Grandad was apparently fast asleep, she had flown to the bird cage hoping to pick up their trail somehow. Straightaway, she'd been able to sense them. They had been happy birds. Chirpy. Well looked after. Full of seed, but a little…empty-headed. She formed the impression that canaries, once lost, would be twittery and confused and not be able to find their way home. They could be anywhere.

At that precise moment, without thinking, she had flicked her tail and it had caught the bell and set it tinkling. The old man had immediately stirred. Glade still had time to whizz back to the table, but in her moment of panic she'd caught sight of herself in the mirror

that hung from the roof of the cage
and had frozen, confusing herself
into thinking she'd been seen.

Then Melanie was in the room
and Grandad was in trouble.

Not too long after that, Glade
found herself where she was now:
stuffed under Melanie's bed.

Later, when Melanie came up, she
pulled Glade out and talked to her
kindly under the covers. Glade was
not terribly good at understanding

human-speak, but Melanie's mood was lighter now and Glade felt happy. Her ivy glowed deep gold. The colour of love.

After twenty minutes of cuddling, Melanie stood Glade on her bedside table and switched off the light. Contented, sleepy sounds soon filled the room.

Time went by and Glade waited patiently. First for the sound of Rachel putting Pops to bed, then for the echoes of darkness: the creaking of the house, the scratching of the wind, an owl hooting somewhere in the distance.

When she was certain everything was safe, Glade softened and flew to the window where Melanie's mother had left an air gap. Within seconds, the young dragon was down in the garden. In her connections with the old man she had sensed his belief in something magical. When he'd scurried down the path with her he hadn't stopped chattering about beings called 'fairies'. He'd been taking Glade to his garden shed to meet them when he'd stumbled and dropped her in the pond! That had ended that adventure, of course. But Glade was determined to find the fairies. Maybe they could tell her where the birds had gone?

The shed door was slightly ajar. Glade fluttered in, landing on a rickety wooden shelf. There was no moonlight, but by letting her ivy glow amber she could light up the place with ease. A range of garden tools were hanging up on nails. There was a watering can on the high shelf opposite and on the shelf below that a jumble of terracotta plant pots and saucers. Glade immediately flew to them. Grandad's mind, she remembered, had been focused on the plant pots, particularly upturned mossy ones.

She found a small pot and peered through the hole in its base. There was nothing to see but shadows. But shadows, Glade knew, often kept secrets. Heart beating, she tilted back the pot, pushed her snout underneath it and hurred a soft "Hello?" Nothing. Just a lovely earthy smell from the gritty red surface. It was the same with the other pots. No fairies.

Hrrr.

But on the end of the shelf, Glade did find something interesting: seeds. Dozens, all the same, in a shallow dish. She dug her paw into them and picked some up, enjoying the sensation of them tumbling through her claws. Unable to resist the urge to grow one, she picked up the smallest plant pot, flew it to a bag of soil on the floor and filled it with earth she was able to scrape from a split in the bag. Then she flew the pot back to the shelf, worked a hole in the soil with her tail and popped the seed in.

Water. All seeds needed water. Lifting the pot carefully, Glade flew it out to the pond. She landed on the small stone island at its centre. There she set the pot down, then made a basin with her paws and dipped them into the motionless pond. The surface rippled, sending out signals to the reedy edge. Glade lifted a scoop of water and drained it into the pot. As the soil softened, she placed her paws around the pot rim and hurred. Before long the soil jiggled and a shoot emerged, frail and tall. Glade's ivy glowed a deep shade of green. She hurred again and the shoot split, producing two heart-shaped stubby leaves. And then, as if that wasn't wonderful

enough, somewhere high above, the
clouds moved and a column of
moonlight visited the garden.

Glade turned her gaze upwards and hurred. The pale grey moon seemed to smile down at her. A soft breeze tickled the surface of the pond. The reeds crackled and all of a sudden Glade felt…a presence.

"Hello, dragon," it said.

Something was here.

Chapter 8

Glade turned solid in an instant.

"It's all right," said 'the presence'. "I know what you are. I saw you moving. I won't tell. Frog's honour."

Frog? Remaining motionless, Glade rolled her eyes sideways and saw a slim green creature with webbed feet and round eyes sitting on a lily pad just a short hop away.

"It's very clever, being able to turn to stone," it said. "Nice trick. I like your plant."

Although Glade wasn't touching it now, the plant was still emerging. She softened her scales and turned to face the frog.

A gulp of air billowed in the sacs in the frog's throat. "You won't eat me, will you? We're a bit rubbery, you know." It crouched back into the water and blinked.

Glade looked around to check that no humans were watching and shook her head.

"Thank you," said the frog. "I thought you looked friendly. I'm

Cecil, by the way. Stupid name for a frog, but there you go. I haven't seen you before. Are you searching for fairies?"

Glade found herself nodding.

"Thought so," Cecil said. He blew a string of bubbles across the water. "They don't come very often. The fairies, I mean. But their magic does. I think it's up there, in the stars."

His eyes popped skyward. The clouds were skimming the moon again.

"That's a fairy stone you're sitting on for sure," he said. "They'll like it that you grew them a plant. If you leave it for them, they'll do something wonderful. Are you going to make a wish? You don't say much, do you?"

Hrrr, went Glade.

"Ooh, erm, ribbit!" Cecil replied. "If we're going to talk posh!"

Glade tightened her eye ridges into a frown. "Make a wish?" she said.

"It's allowed, if you stand on the stone in the moonlight."

"Have you tried it?" Glade asked him, flicking her tail.

Cecil bloated his chest. "I've got everything I need," he said. "My pond. My reeds. Mrs Cecil. We'll have tadpoles soon."

Glade wasn't sure she understood this, but she smiled anyway.

"Go on," he said, puffing his rubbery cheeks, "wish for anything you like. Fairy moon magic is very strong."

Glade tapped her foot and thought about her mission. "I wish Melanie's canaries would come home."

Cecil sat up in the water. "Now you have to turn. Turn three times or it doesn't work." He stirred the pond with his foot.

So Glade lifted her tail and, being careful not to knock her plant pot over, turned three times.

Apart from the fact that she now felt dizzy, nothing much seemed to have happened.

Then, suddenly, a light went on in the house. Glade gasped and her

heart scales rattled. Fortunately, the light wasn't from Melanie's room. Glade blew a smoke ring in relief.

"I have to go," she said, spreading her wings.

"I'll guard the plant," said Cecil.

The main stem had now grown as high as Glade's ears. Already there were four slim branches, each with six leaves.

Glade blew a smoke perfect ring. Someone was going to see that and wonder how it had got there. But if Cecil was correct about the fairies, then it was only right to leave it as a gift. "Do you know what kind of plant it is?" she asked him.

"Oh yes," he said. "Rub a leaf between your paws."

Glade tried it. The leaf felt crisp and new.

"Now hold your paws to your snout and sniff."

And when she did, Glade had the most pleasant surprise.

Her paws smelled beautifully of lemons.

Chapter 9

The next morning, Liz received a phone call from Rachel.

"Something extraordinary has happened," said Rachel. "I'd like you to see it. Can you come round?"

Knowing better than to spoil a surprise by asking too soon what it was, Liz replied, "Yes, of course. I'm just popping out to the shops. We'll call in on the way back."

Lucy raised her eyes from her breakfast bowl. "Is that Rachel? Is Glade OK?"

Liz put the phone down. "Glade knows how to look after herself. But it sounds like she might have been up to something."

"Something?" said Lucy, fishing for details.

"Mmm. Put your coat on and we'll go and find out."

* * *

A few minutes later, they were on their way to the small convenience store just around the corner from

98

Wayward Crescent where it joined the main Scrubbley Road. It was run by a man called Mr Calhoun. It sold everything from bananas to batteries.

Lucy was beside herself with impatience. "Can't we go straight to Melanie's?" she tutted, slouching along with her hands in her pockets. "We can do the shoping afterwards, can't we?"

"This is important," said Liz. She flapped a piece of card in Lucy's face.

"What's that?"

"An advert."

ADVERTISEMENT
LOST. Two canaries.
Any information please
ring: Scrubbley 01427824
* REWARD *

"Are we selling something?"

"No."

The shop door rattled as Liz walked in. Mr Calhoun, a ginger-haired man with a lopsided mouth, raised a wispy eyebrow to her. He was famous for saying little and grunting a lot.

"Morning, Eric," Liz greeted him cheerily.

Mr Calhoun wiped his hands on his apron. Lucy hated his apron. It smelled of cheese.

"I'd like to put this in your window, please." Liz handed him the card.

Mr Calhoun held it at arm's length to read it. True to form, he grunted.

"For one week," said Liz. "How much will that be?"

This should be fun, thought Lucy. *He's going to have to speak.*

Mr Calhoun, however, looked at the ceiling. Lucy followed his gaze, but could see nothing but a damp patch on the polystyrene tiles.

Saying not a word, Mr Calhoun stepped out from behind his counter and strolled down the aisle of tinned veg and meat. He crooked a finger, beckoning Liz and Lucy to follow. They reached the shop window, where he swung out a board containing many more adverts. Without explanation, he tore one away from its drawing pin and handed it to Liz. Then he walked silently back behind his counter, scratching the seat of his trousers all the way.

"Oh, he is so rude," Lucy huffed.

"He's actually very kind – when you get to know him," Liz said. "Come on. We're going to Arkle Road."

"What?!" Arkle Road was near Lucy's school. It was back towards Melanie's, but still out of their way.

Then Liz showed her the advert.

'FOUND' it said in black capital letters.

"Oh," said Lucy.

"Quite," said Liz.

On the card was a picture of two canaries.

* * *

And so it was that some twenty minutes later, Liz and Lucy arrived at number 7, Orchid Close with a new friend. She was an elderly lady called Agnes Murray, grey-haired and trim, with lively blue eyes. She wore a bright orange coat with large black buttons. She looked like a well-wrapped sweet.

Rachel opened the door. Liz was about to do the explanations when Melanie burst into the hall and panted, "Mum, he's started pulling them up!"

Lucy caught her breath. Melanie had Glade in her hands.

Rachel beckoned everyone in. They pursued Melanie through the house and into the garden.

Pops was in his dressing gown, pulling up weeds. They were everywhere – in the borders, the planters, popping out of the drain, even in bare patches on the lawn. There were dozens by the pond. Pops was going after every single one.

"I can't understand it," Rachel sighed. "They sprang up overnight. How can that happen?"

Agnes Murray picked up a loose stem. "Have you noticed they're all the same, my dear?"

"Are they? Oh, yes," said Rachel, looking around. That just seemed to confuse her even more.

Agnes rubbed a leaf. "Lemon balm," she said, smelling her fingers.

"A cleansing herb. Excellent for bringing clarity of mind."

"Lemon balm?" said Rachel. "But that's…"

Liz smiled at Agnes and looked down the garden where Pops had suddenly stopped pulling the 'weeds'. Now he too was smelling his hands. He swayed a little and sank down onto a bench. He blinked a few times and tried to speak. Then he looked at Melanie, and he started to cry.

"Oh, Grandad! Whatever's the matter?" she said. She hurried down the garden to sit beside him.

Rachel was about to follow, but Liz put a hand on her arm and held her back.

Grandad took Melanie's hands in his.

"Are you poorly? Shall we get a doctor?" she asked.

"No, pet," he said. "I'm all right, I think."

Rachel gasped lightly and covered her mouth. "He's not called her 'pet' for years," she whispered.

Melanie touched her grandad's

cheek. "Why are you crying?"

"Because of the birds."

"Oh," said Melanie. She stared at her feet.

"Didn't mean it," said Pops. "Wasn't thinking straight when I let them escape."

"I know," she said.

He squeezed her hand. "I miss them. I was sad they went."

"Mmm," said Melanie. She tried not to sniff.

"But what made it even sadder was that I couldn't find the words to say sorry to you."

"Mmm," went Melanie. This time it was a squeak.

Grandad sniffed the lemon balm again. "But somehow, today, I can."

Melanie dripped a tear on Glade. It ran like a small pearl over her heart. No one seemed to notice that Glade's ivy had begun to glow a deep shade of blue. "Perhaps it was dragon magic, Grandad?"

He put a thumb on Glade's snout, just under her eye. "Aye, pet, perhaps it was. You know, if I didn't know better, I'd say this dragon was going to—"

"Cry!" said Lucy, stealing Glade out of Melanie's arms.

"Hey!" shouted Melanie, standing up to face her.

"It's all right, Glade, we found the birds!" said Lucy.

"The canaries?" gasped Rachel.

Liz gestured to Agnes.

"They flew into my conservatory two weeks ago," said Agnes. "They've been keeping Alfie, my budgerigar, company. I put a postcard in Calhoun's window. I didn't know what else to do. Today, by some means – or magic – all is well."

"You see," Lucy whispered in dragontongue to Glade. "All is well. Please don't cry your fire tear. Please."

"Excuse me," said Melanie. "Why are you coughing in my dragon's face?" With a slight *hmph*, she snatched Glade back.

"She isn't," said Liz, weaving the words like a silken spell. "She's talking to Glade in an ancient language called dragontongue. You must never let a dragon cry. If you do, it can never work its magic again."

"Really?" Melanie's mouth fell open.

There was a pause, then Rachel hooted, "For goodness' sake, Liz. You almost had me believing you for a moment. Come on, let's go inside and…have a cup of tea!"

Everyone, even Grandad, burst out laughing.

And to Lucy's relief, Glade's ivy was glowing gold.

Chapter 10

"Are we really going to leave Glade with them?" asked Lucy as she helped her mother do the drying up. It had been two days since the drama in the garden at Orchid Close. The two canaries had been returned, Melanie's grandad was feeling a lot better, he and Agnes had become good friends, and so far there had been no more worrying calls from Rachel.

But a special dragon was a special dragon. Lucy couldn't help but feel anxious.

"She'll be fine," said Liz. "She's learned an awful lot in the past few days. She's happy where she is. Besides, if she's ever in trouble, she can always send a message to the listening dragon."

Lucy glanced at the dragon on the fridge. It stretched its ears and hurred politely.

"So was it Glade who

made all those lemon plants grow?"

Liz polished a fork and put it in the drawer. She stared out across the sunlit garden and smiled. "I think she might have had a little help."

"From fairies? I thought there was no such thing?"

"Some people would say the same about dragons, Lucy."

"Hmm," she went, and stuffed her tea towel into a cup. "Will the plants stop Melanie's grandad from dying?"

"I don't think that's the point," said Liz. "What really mattered, to both of them, was that Pops was able to say sorry for what he'd done. Glade helped him to achieve that. Mission accomplished."

"It was us who found the canaries, though," Lucy said proudly.

"Or we were shown where to look," said Liz. She hung up her towel. "Maybe we had some fairy help, too. Trust me, there are lots of mysteries in this world. Which reminds me, I've had a strange idea."

She walked down the hall and opened the door to the spare room. "One that will make us a bit more money."

Lucy raised a sceptical eyebrow. "Are you going to sell special dragons for one hundred pounds each?"

"No. I thought we might have a lodger one day. A student from Scrubbley College, perhaps."

Lucy's mouth went as wide as a bucket. A lodger? An outsider? Someone who probably didn't even believe in dragons, actually coming to live in their house?

"We'd have to clear this lot out, of course." Liz nodded at the piles of junk in the room.

Lucy blinked and banged the side of her head. "But, Mum, they'd be normal. We can't have normal people living in our house. Not with the dragons flying about."

Liz folded her arms and looked thoughtfully at the room. A bed by the window and a decent pair of curtains. It could work. "You never know, things might be different one day."

Lucy gave a curt *humph*. "I want a cat."

Liz shook her head. "Absolutely no cats."

"Absolutely no lodgers!" Lucy said stubbornly.

"One day, things might be different," Liz repeated, as if she was talking to an unseen ghost. She closed the door quietly and patted it once.

One day.

Maybe the fairies would decide.

Here's an extract from
the next story about

The Dragons of Wayward Crescent

GRABBER

978 1 40830 235 4 £8.99 (hb)
978 1 84616 612 9 £4.99 (pbk)

This story begins on a dark and stormy night. Well, actually, that's not strictly true. It was definitely dark, but not exactly stormy. Though it probably should have been. For this is a tale of dreadful villainy. Of foul play, wickedness and shameful wrongdoings. It's the story of a man who ought to have known better.

And that man's name is Ron the robber.

It all takes place in the sleepy town of Scrubbley, on a quiet leafy road called Wayward Crescent. Most of the people who live in this Crescent are perfectly ordinary, respectable folks. But as some of you will know, the house towards the end, at number 42, is owned by a woman called Elizabeth Pennykettle – 'Liz' to her neighbours, 'Mum' to her nine-year-old daughter, Lucy.

Now, though she's respectable, Liz is not entirely ordinary. She makes dragons, clay dragons, which she sells on the market. There's nothing very strange about that, of course. But every now and then, when a magical mood inspires her, Liz makes a special kind of dragon. One that might look like a normal solid sculpture, but is in fact real. Very, very real.

This is how it was on the night that Ron the robber broke into Liz's house. She had just made a new special dragon. A handsome young male. At that time his special abilities were not known. And he had no name.

Liz had left him on her potter's

turntable, in her workroom upstairs which she called the Dragons' Den, while she and Lucy had gone out for the evening. The new dragon was in the care of a female called Guinevere. Guinevere was Liz's personal dragon and she was *very* special indeed. It was Guinevere's job to 'awaken' the young dragons when they were made. How she did it was a secret, and the details are not to be written down here. All that matters for the moment is that the dragon on the turntable could blink and blow smoke rings and swish his tail. He was eager to test his wings as well. For there was lots to explore in the Dragons' Den. The window that looked out onto the garden, for instance. And the shelves of fascinating dragon sculptures. But Guinevere had spoken firmly to him in dragontongue, telling him he must await Liz's return before trying out his flying skills. Young dragons, she had said, had much to learn.

So, there we have it. The scene is set. As the sun goes down and the Dragons' Den falls into dusky shadow, picture the young dragon sitting and waiting, drumming his claws on the wooden turntable, warming the air with a *hrrr* now and then.

Then, suddenly, his ears prick up. For somewhere far below he has heard a sound. A gentle crash. A sharp sort of tinkle. He is too young to know about the layout of the house or that the sound is a small pane of glass breaking in the kitchen door. But he sits up eagerly, expectantly, keenly, wondering if this means his mistress is coming.

Just then, however, another young dragon swoops into the den. This is Gruffen. He is a guard dragon, made to protect Lucy Pennykettle from danger. But Lucy is not here. She is in no danger. But Gruffen is concerned that the house might be. As he lands on the table next to Guinevere he tells her what he has seen. He was on the kitchen table when the glass was broken. He saw a gloved hand fiddle through the hole and turn the key which was sitting in the lock. He saw the door open and a man step in. Not Henry, the Pennykettles' next door neighbour. A stranger. A stranger dressed like the night. Sturdy black boots. Black jacket. Black hat. A stranger carrying a flashing torch.

Guinevere urges him to search through his book. (Gruffen has a book which he always carries with him, a kind of manual of dragon procedures.) By the light of Guinevere's violet flame, he looks up the word 'strangers'. The new young dragon leans forward to watch. This is very exciting! He wonders if life here is always like this?

There is an entry in the book, but it is not very helpful. '*In the presence of strangers, act solid*' it says. This is a rule all the special dragons know – except for those just born, of course.

There is a creak on the landing. A footstep. Two. Light breaks at steep angles into the Den. Gruffen and Guinevere immediately turn solid, forgetting that the youngster doesn't know what to do.

A figure steps in. He is short. A little brawny. Stubble on the fatty parts of his chin. The light twists and burrs around the shelves, making soft glints as it catches on the ears and tails of clay.

"Well, well, what 'ave we 'ere?" the figure says. A man. Soft-spoken. Quite elderly, perhaps. With slightly yellow teeth. And slightly fishy breath.

The light flips again, towards the table. It passes over Guinevere. It passes over Gruffen. But when it hits the new dragon, he sits up and *hrrrs…*

GAUGE

978 1 40830 233 0 £8.99 (hb)
978 1 84616 610 5 £4.99 (pbk)

About the Author

Chris d'Lacey originally wanted to be a songwriter, and only started writing books when a friend suggested he entered a competition to write a children's story. Since then Chris has had over twenty books published, including *Fly, Cherokee, Fly*, which was highly commended for the Carnegie Medal.

In July 2002 he was awarded an honourary doctorate by the University of Leicester for his services to children's fiction. Chris is married and lives in Leicester, England. You can read more about him by visiting his website: www.icefire.co.uk

More books by Chris d'Lacey

The Fire Within
Chris d'Lacey   978 1 84121 533 4   £5.99

Icefire
Chris d'Lacey   978 1 84362 134 8   £5.99

Fire Star
Chris d'Lacey   978 1 84362 522 3   £5.99

The Fire Eternal
Chris d'Lacey   978 1 84616 426 2   £5.99

Dark Fire
Chris d'Lacey   978 1 84616 955 7   £6.99

Orchard Books are available from all good bookshops, or can be ordered from our website: www.orchardbooks.co.uk, or telephone 01235 827 702, or fax 01235 827 703